NURSE LUGTON'S CURTAIN

BY VIRGINIA WOOLF

Illustrated by Julie Vivas

THE BODLEY HEAD

LONDON

NURSE LUGTON was asleep. She had given one great snore. She had dropped her head; thrust her spectacles up her forehead; and there she sat by the fender with her finger sticking up and a thimble on it; and her needle full of cotton hanging down; and she was snoring, snoring; and on her knees, covering the whole of her apron, was a large piece of figured blue stuff.

The animals with which it was covered did not move till
Nurse Lugton snored for the fifth time. One, two, three, four,
five — ah, the old woman was at last asleep. The antelope
nodded to the zebra; the giraffe bit through the leaf on the
tree top; all the animals began to toss and prance.

For the pattern on the blue stuff was made of troops of wild beasts and below them was a lake and a bridge and a town with round roofs and little men and women looking out of the windows and riding over the bridge on horseback.

But directly the old nurse snored for the fifth time, the blue stuff turned to blue air; the trees waved; you could hear the water of the lake breaking; and see the people moving over the bridge and waving their hands out of the windows.

The animals now began to move. First went the elephant
and the zebra; next the giraffe and the tiger; the ostrich, the
mandrill, twelve marmots and a pack of mongeese followed;
the penguins and the pelicans waddled and waded, often
pecking at each other, alongside.

Over them burnt Nurse Lugton's golden thimble like a sun; and as Nurse Lugton snored, the animals heard the wind roaring through the forest. Down they went to drink, and as they trod, the blue curtain (for Nurse Lugton was making a curtain for Mrs John Jasper Gingham's drawing-room window) became made of grass, and roses and daisies; strewn with white and black stones; with puddles on it, and cart tracks, and little frogs hopping quickly lest the elephants should tread on them. Down they went, down the hill to the lake to drink.

And soon all were gathered on the edge of the lake, some stooping down, others throwing their heads up.

Really, it was a beautiful sight —

and to think of all this lying across old Nurse Lugton's knees while she slept, sitting on her Windsor chair in the lamplight — to think of her apron covered with roses and grass, and with all these wild beasts trampling on it, when Nurse Lugton was mortally afraid even of poking through the bars with her umbrella at the Zoo! Even a little black beetle made her jump. But Nurse Lugton slept; Nurse Lugton saw nothing at all.

The elephants drank; and the giraffes snipped off the leaves on the highest tulip trees; and the people who crossed the bridges threw bananas at them, and tossed pineapples up into the air, and beautiful golden rolls stuffed with quinces and rose leaves, for the monkeys loved them.

The old Queen came by in her palanquin; the general of the
army passed; so did the Prime Minister; the Admiral, the
Executioner; and great dignitaries on business in the town,
which was a very beautiful place called Millamarchmantopolis.

Nobody harmed the lovely beasts; many pitied them; for it was well known that even the smallest monkey was enchanted. For a great ogress had them in her toils, the people knew; and the great ogress was called Lugton.

They could see her, from their windows, towering over them. She had a face like the side of a mountain with great precipices and avalanches, and chasms for her eyes and hair and nose and teeth. And every animal which strayed into her territories she froze alive, so that all day they stood stock still on her knee, but when she fell asleep, then they were released, and down they came in the evening to Millamarchmantopolis to drink.

Suddenly old Nurse Lugton twitched the curtain all in crinkles. For a big bluebottle was buzzing round the lamp, and woke her. Up she sat and stuck her needle in.

The animals flashed back in a second. The air became
blue stuff.

And the curtain lay quite still on her knee. Nurse Lugton took up her needle, and went on sewing Mrs Gingham's drawing-room curtain.

First published in the United States of America in 1991
by Harcourt Brace Jovanovich, Inc.

First published in 1991 by The Bodley Head Children's Books
an imprint of The Random Century Group Ltd
20 Vauxhall Bridge Road, London SW1V 2SA

Random Century Australia (Pty) Ltd
20 Alfred Street, Sydney, NSW 2061

Random Century New Zealand Ltd
PO Box 40-086, Glenfield, Auckland 10, New Zealand

Random Century South Africa (Pty) Ltd
PO Box 337, Bergvlei 2012, South Africa

Printed and bound by Tien Wah Press, Singapore

British Cataloguing in Publication Data is Available

ISBN 0 370 31519 7